A. FRANK SMITH. JR. LIBRARY CENTER
SOUTHWESTERN UNIVERSITY
GEORGETOWN. TEXAS 78626

A. FRANK SMITH, JR. LIBRARY CENTER
SOUTHWESTERN UNIVERSITY

3 3053 00262 9921

DATE DUE

W9-CML-525

WINDS
AND
WILDCAT
PLACES

 KODANSHA INTERNATIONAL LTD.
Tokyo, Japan   Palo Alto, Calif. U.S.A.

WINDS
AND
WILDCAT
PLACES

Stories by

KENJI MIYAZAWA

translation by John Bester

illustrations by Rokurō Taniuchi

DISTRIBUTORS:

British Commonwealth (excluding Canada and the Far East)
WARD LOCK & COMPANY LTD.
London and Melbourne

France
HACHETTE—LIBRAIRIE ETRANGERE
Paris

Continental Europe (excluding France)
BOXERBOOKS, INC.
Zurich

The Far East
JAPAN PUBLICATIONS TRADING COMPANY
C.P.O. Box 722, Tokyo

Published by KODANSHA INTERNATIONAL LTD., 2-12-21, Otowa, Bunkyo-ku, Tokyo, Japan and KODANSHA INTERNATIONAL/USA, LTD., 577 College Avenue, Palo Alto, California 94306. Copyright © 1967, by KODANSHA INTERNATIONAL LTD. All rights reserved. Printed in Japan.
Library of Congress Catalog Card No. 67-26309
First edition, 1967

CF
M699w

Table of Contents

To the Reader 7

Wildcat and the Acorns 11

The Restaurant of Many Orders 25

Nighthawk and the Stars 38

The First Deer Dance 50

The Earth-god and the Fox 64

The Red Blanket 84

To
the
Reader

The man who wrote the stories in this book was born and lived all his life in Japan. If you were to read them before you knew anything about the author, you might be rather surprised to hear this. Even nowadays, many people somehow feel that Japan is a very distant—or at least, a very different—country from their own. If you have read stories about Japan in other books, you almost certainly found them full of unfamiliar ways of thinking and living and feeling.

You might be surprised, then, because you will find almost nothing here that might not have happened to you, or that you might not have felt yourself. There is no sense at all that you are in a strange land. Yet it *is* a strange land—except that the strangeness has nothing to do with traveling, or with foreign countries. It's the same strangeness, the same sense of excitement and wonder, that is here all around us from the beginning, in the sunshine and the breeze, in the stars and the storms, waiting for us behind every bush on the paths we walk when we are young.

Since he loved books himself, Kenji Miyazawa had of course read a great deal about other countries, and had read books written in other countries, too. But in all other ways, in his work and in the way he lived, he could hardly have been closer to his own native soil. His life was spent in the north of Japan's main island, in a district where the people are poor and the winters hard. He knew the long months when everything is buried under the snow, the yearly surprise of spring, the blazing colors of summer, and the cool, clear autumn days when the mountains are blue and the trees red and gold and the silver grasses wave on the plain.

Since he spent most of his days studying techniques and ways of farming, working hand-in-hand with the farmers in their struggle to make their lot a little easier, he naturally lived in close touch with the four seasons. But unlike some people who live so close to Nature that they never notice it, he never seems to have stopped wondering at its beauty, its color, and its mystery.

He noticed everything, from the ant crawling at his feet and the quivering of the leaves on the trees to the Milky Way stretching pale across the sky in the far, far distance. And back at home at nights—perhaps on those same nights that the Old Snow Woman and her followers were raging about outside—he would write poems and stories about what he had seen and felt. Then the colors of Nature would blaze again on the

8

paper before him almost as though he was holding a paintbrush rather than a pen, and under the spell of his imagination, the fields and forests he loved would come alive with wildcats and foxes, frogs and deer, and a crowd of other creatures.

Even the trees and hills, the gentle breeze and the howling gale, were all living creatures for him, and he gave them speech in just the same way as the human beings in his tales. And through that speech he tried to do something else, too—to express one small part of all the things he had thought and felt, as he went about his work, about people and the way they behave.

Perhaps it is just because he lived, in a way, such a simple life that the things he says to us through the mouths of his creatures often seem to touch on something inside us that we all have but lose sight of once we forget what it is to be young. That is one reason—though you may not see it all at once—why his stories really belong not only to Japan but to all of us.

It is already thirty-four years since he died, at the age of thirty-seven. At the time of his death, all that most people knew of his work was some of his poems and a few of his stories, including some of those in this book. But he had written much more, and friends who loved his work collected it together and had it published in book form. Before long, many people all over Japan—not only children, but grownups too—were reading his poems and stories, and he soon came to have a special place all his own in Japanese literature.

As time goes on, I hope that something will stay with

you from these stories, and that you will turn back to them from time to time. Not, of course, that they set out to "teach" you something terribly serious. They are all good stories, with a proper beginning, middle, and end, as all good stories should have, and you can enjoy them as much now as you ever will. But under the surface they don't really belong to any time of life, any more than they belong to any particular country. However long we live, the grass will always grow at our feet and the stars hang over our heads, and standing between them we shall sometimes feel rather frightened. Miyazawa, too, knew how it was to be frightened by the world about him, but he managed to love it at the same time, and to love his fellow-creatures as well.

Sometimes in the years to come you may know the sense of wonder that Kaju had when he joined the deer in worshiping the sun on that magical autumn day of the story. At other times, you may feel something of the despair of the nighthawk as he circled the skies between the forest fire down below and the stars above. Sometimes you may even feel that, in actual life, Kaju could never really have become one with Nature and danced with the deer in the setting sun, or that nighthawks never really go up to the heavens and become stars. But what matters still more—Miyazawa seems to say—is to feel, and to try, for this is where we are, and this is what we have, and things as they are can be very beautiful, too.

JOHN BESTER

10

Wildcat

and

the Acorns

One Saturday evening, a most peculiar postcard arrived at Ichiro's house. This is what it said:

> *Mr. Ichiro Kaneta*   *September 19*
> *Pleased to know as how you're well. Tomorrow I've got a difficult case to judge, so please come. Please don't bring no firearms.*
>
>   *Yours respectfully,*
>   *Wildcat*

That was all. The writing was terrible, and the ink so blobby it nearly stuck to your fingers. But Ichiro was beside himself with joy. He put the card in his satchel when no one was looking and took it to school, and all day long he was bouncing up and down with delight.

Even after he'd crept into bed that night, he still kept imagining Wildcat's face with its cat's grin, and the scene at tomorrow's trial, and so many other things that he couldn't sleep until quite late.

When he awoke, though, it was already broad daylight. He went outside, and there were the hills lined up beneath a bright blue sky, rising as fresh and clean as though they'd just been made. He hurried through his breakfast and set off alone upstream, up the path by the stream in the valley. Each time there came a gust of wind from the fresh morning breeze, the chestnut trees showered their nuts in all directions. Ichiro looked up at them.

"Chestnut trees, chestnut trees," he called. "Did Wildcat pass this way?"

And the chestnut trees paused a while in their rustling, and replied:

"Wildcat? Yes, he rushed past in a carriage early this morning, going to the east."

"The east? That's the way I'm going. How strange! At any rate, I'll keep on this way and see. Thank you, chestnut trees."

The chestnut trees made no answer, but went on scattering their nuts in all directions. So Ichiro went a little farther, and came to the Flute Falls. They were called the Flute Falls because there was a small hole about halfway up a pure white cliff, through which the water spurted whistling like a flute before becoming a waterfall and dropping with a roar into the valley below. Facing the waterfall, Ichiro shouted up at it.

"Hello there, Flute Falls! Did Wildcat pass this way?"

12

"Wildcat?" replied the waterfall in a high, whistly voice. "Yes, he rushed past in a carriage a while ago, going to the west."

"The west?" said Ichiro. "That's the way my home is. How strange! Anyway, I'll go a bit farther and see. Thank you, waterfall."

But the waterfall was already whistling to itself as it always did. So Ichiro went a little farther, and came to a beech-tree. Under the tree, a crowd of white mushrooms were playing in a strange kind of orchestra: tiddley-tum-tum, tiddley-tum-tum! Ichiro bent down towards them.

"Hello, mushrooms," he said. "Did Wildcat pass this way?"

"Wildcat?" replied the mushrooms. "Yes, he rushed past in a carriage early this morning, going to the south."

"That's strange," said Ichiro, racking his brains. "That's in those mountains over there. Anyway, I'll go a bit farther and see. Thank you, mushrooms."

But the mushrooms were already busy again, playing their strange music: tiddley-tum-tum, tiddley-tum-tum. . .

Ichiro was walking on, when he noticed a squirrel hopping about in the branches of a walnut tree.

"You, squirrel!" called Ichiro, beckoning to him to stop. "Did Wildcat pass this way?"

"Wildcat?" said the squirrel, shading his eyes with a paw as he peered down at Ichiro. "Yes, he rushed past this morning in a carriage, going to the south."

"The south?" said Ichiro. "That's strange—that's twice I've been told that. Ah well, I'll go a bit farther and see. Thank you, squirrel."

But the squirrel had gone. All that he could see was the topmost branches of the walnut tree swaying a little, and the leaves of the neighboring beech-tree flashing for a moment in the sun.

A little farther on, and the path along the stream grew narrower, then disappeared altogether. There was a small new path, however, leading up towards the dark wood to the south of the stream, so Ichiro set off up it. The branches of the trees were heavy and densely packed, and not the tiniest patch of blue sky was to be seen. The path became steeper and steeper. Ichiro's face turned bright red, and the sweat fell in great drops. Suddenly, though, he came out into the light. He had reached a beautiful golden meadow. The grass rustled in the breeze, and all around stood fine, olive-colored trees.

There, in the middle of the meadow, a most odd-looking little man was watching Ichiro. He was squatting down, and in his hand he held a leather whip. Ichiro slowly went nearer to him, then stopped in astonishment. The little man was one-eyed, and his blind eye, which was white, kept moving. His legs were very bandy, like a goat's, and—most peculiar of all—his feet were shaped like spades.

"Do you happen to know Wildcat?" Ichiro asked, trying not to show his nervousness. The little man looked at Ichiro with his one eye and his mouth twisted into a leer.

"Mr. Wildcat will be back in just a moment," he said. "You'll be Ichiro, I suppose?"

Ichiro started back in astonishment.

"Yes, I'm Ichiro," he replied. "But how did you know?"

The strange little man gave an even broader leer.

"Then you got the postcard?" he asked.

"Yes, that's why I came," Ichiro said.

"Terribly bad style, wasn't it?" asked the little man, looking gloomily down at the ground. Ichiro felt sorry for him.

"No," he said. "It seemed very good to me."

The little man gasped for joy and blushed to the tips of his ears. He pulled his coat open at the neck to cool himself, and asked:

"Was the writing very good too?"

Ichiro couldn't help smiling.

"Very good," he said, "I doubt if even a fifth-grader could write that well."

The little man's face suddenly looked depressed again.

"When you say fifth-grader, you mean at primary school, I suppose?" His voice was so listless and pathetic that Ichiro was alarmed.

"Oh, no," he said hastily. "At university."

The little man cheered up again, and grinned so broadly that his face seemed to be all mouth.

"I wrote that postcard," he shouted.

"Just who are you, then?" asked Ichiro, trying not to smile.

"I am Mr. Wildcat's coachman!" he replied.

16

A sudden gust of wind rippled over the grass, and the coachman gave a deep bow. Puzzled, Ichiro turned round, and there was Wildcat, standing behind him. He wore a fine, yellow brocade coat, and his green eyes as he stared at Ichiro were perfectly round. Ichiro barely had time to note that his ears were pointed and stuck up just like an ordinary cat's, when Wildcat gave a stiff little bow.

"Oh, good morning," said Ichiro politely, bowing in return. "Thank you for the postcard."

"Good morning," said Wildcat, pulling his whiskers out stiff and sticking out his chest. "I'm pleased to see you. The fact is, a most troublesome dispute arose the day before yesterday, and I don't quite know how to judge it, so I thought I might ask your opinion. But at any rate, make yourself at home, won't you? The acorns should be here at any moment now. Really, you know, I have a lot of trouble with this trial every year."

He took a cigarette case from inside his coat, and put a cigarette in his mouth.

"Won't you have one?" he said, and offered the case to Ichiro.

"Oh, no thank you," said Ichiro, startled.

"Ho, ho! Of course, you're still young," said Wildcat with a lordly kind of laugh. He struck a match and, screwing up his face self-consciously, puffed out a cloud of blue smoke. His coachman, who was standing by stiffly awaiting orders, seemed to be dying for a cigarette himself, for big tears were rolling down his face.

Just then, Ichiro heard a tiny crackling sound at his

17

feet, like salt being put on the fire. He bent down in surprise to look, and saw that the ground was covered with little round gold things, all twinkling away in the grass. When he looked closer, he could see they were acorns—there must have been over three hundred of them—all wearing red trousers and all chattering away about something at the tops of their voices.

"Here they come! Just like a lot of ants," said Wildcat, throwing away his cigarette. "You there, ring the bell," he hurriedly ordered the coachman. "And cut the grass just there, where it's sunny."

The coachman took a big sickle from his side, and feverishly swished down the grass in front of Wildcat. Immediately, the acorns came rushing out from the grass on all sides, glittering in the sun as they came, and began to set up a clamor.

The coachman rang his bell. Clang, clang! it went. Clang, clang! the sound echoed through the woods, and the golden acorns became a little quieter. Unnoticed by Ichiro, Wildcat had put on a long black satin gown, and was now sitting looking important in front of the acorns. It reminded Ichiro of pictures he had seen of crowds of tiny worshipers before a great, bronze idol.

Swish, crack! swish, crack! went the coachman with his whip. The sky was blue and cloudless, and the acorns sparkled most beautifully.

"Don't you know this is the third day this case has been going on?" Wildcat began. "How about calling it off and making things up with each other?"

His voice was a little worried, but he forced himself

to sound important. No sooner had he spoken, however, than all the acorns set up a commotion.

"No, it won't do! Whatever you say, the one with the most pointed head is best. And it's me who's the most pointed."

"No, you're wrong, the roundest one's best. I'm the roundest!"

"It's size, I tell you! The biggest one's the best. I'm the biggest, so I'm the best!"

"You're wrong there! I'm much bigger. Don't you remember the judge said so yesterday?"

"You're all wrong! It's the one who's the tallest. The tallest one, I tell you!"

"No, it's the one who's best at pushing and shoving. That's what settles it!"

All the acorns were chattering so noisily that in the end you had absolutely no idea what it was all about. It was just like stirring up a hornets' nest.

"That's enough," Wildcat bawled. "Where do you think you are! Be quiet! Be quiet!"

Swish, crack! went the coachman's whip, and at last the acorns were still.

"Don't you know this is the third day this trial has been going on?" demanded Wildcat, twisting his whiskers till they stood on end. "How about calling it off and making things up?"

"No, no, it's no good. Whatever you say, the one with the most pointed head's best."

"No, you're wrong. The roundest one's best!"

"No he's not, it's the biggest!"

Chatter, chatter, chatter again, till you had no idea what it was all about.

"Enough! Where do you think you are!" Wildcat shouted. "Be quiet! Be quiet!"

Swish, crack! went the coachman's whip again. Wildcat twisted his whiskers till they stood on end, then started again.

"Don't you know this is the third day this case has been going on? Why don't you call it off and make things up!"

"No, no, it's no good! The one with the most pointed head . . ." Chatter, chatter chatter . . .

"That's enough!" Wildcat shouted again. "Where do you think you are! Be quiet! Be quiet!"

Again the coachman's whip went swish, crack! and the acorns fell silent once more.

"You see what it's like," whispered Wildcat to Ichiro. "What do you think I ought to do?"

Ichiro smiled.

"Well, then, how about giving a verdict like this?" he said. "Tell them that the best is the one who's most stupid, most ridiculous and most good-for-nothing. I heard it in a sermon, you know."

Wildcat nodded wisely, and prepared to give his verdict. With an enormous air of importance, he pulled open his satin gown at the neck so that the yellow brocade coat showed a little. Then he spoke.

"Right! Be quiet now! Here is my verdict. The best of you is the one who is least important, most foolish,

20

most ridiculous, absolutely good-for-nothing, and completely crack-brained!"

A hush fell over the acorns, a complete hush so that you could have heard a pin drop.

Wildcat took off his black satin gown and, wiping the sweat from his forehead, took Ichiro's hand, while the coachman cracked his whip five or six times for sheer joy.

"I'm most obliged to you," said Wildcat to Ichiro. "I must say, you've taken a most awkward case off my hands in not so much as a minute and a half. I do hope you'll act as honorary judge for my court in future. If ever I send you a postcard from now on, please come, won't you? I'll see you're suitably rewarded every time."

"Of course I'll come," said Ichiro. "But I don't want any reward."

"Oh no," objected Wildcat. "You *must* accept a reward. It's a matter of honor for me, you see. And from now on, I'll address the postcard Ichiro Kaneta, Esq., and call this 'the Court'—is that all right?"

"That's fine," said Ichiro.

Wildcat was silent for a moment, twirling his whiskers as though there was something more he wanted to say. Then he seemed to take courage, and went on:

"And about the wording of the card, you know—how would it be if I put it like this: 'Pertaining to certain business in hand, your presence in court is formally requested'?"

Ichiro smiled.

"It seems a little funny to me, somehow," he said. "Perhaps you'd better leave that bit out, at any rate."

Wildcat gazed crestfallen at the ground, still twiddling

his whiskers, as if regretting that he hadn't put it better. Finally, with a sigh, he went on:

"Well, then, we'll leave it as it stands. Oh yes—and about your reward for today—which do you prefer, a pint of gold acorns or a salted-salmon head?"

"The gold acorns, please," replied Ichiro.

Wildcat straightway turned to the coachman, as if relieved that it hadn't been the salmon head.

"Go and get a pint of gold acorns," he said, speaking fast. "If there aren't enough, you can put in some gold-plated ones. And be quick!"

The coachman began to scoop the acorns into a measure. When he had finished, he gave a shout. "Just a pint," he said.

Wildcat's brocade coat flapped in the breeze. He stretched, closed his eyes, and smothered a yawn.

"Right!" he said. "Now hurry and get the coach ready."

A carriage made of a great white mushroom appeared, drawn by a horse of a most peculiar shape, and gray, just like a rat. Wildcat turned to Ichiro.

"Well, now we'll see you home," he said.

They got into the carriage, and the coachman put the measure full of acorns in beside them. Swish, crack! and off they went. The meadow was left behind, and trees and bushes swayed by in a misty blue. Ichiro's eyes were fixed on his gold acorns, and Wildcat was gazing quite innocently into the distance.

But as the carriage went on, the acorns lost their glitter, and when—in no time, it seemed—the carriage came to a halt, they were just the plain, ordinary, brown kind. Wildcat's yellow brocade coat, and the coachman, and the mushroom carriage—all had vanished together, and Ichiro was left standing before his own home, the measure of acorns in his hand.

From that time on, there were no more postcards signed "Yours respectfully, Wildcat." Ichiro sometimes wonders about it. Perhaps he ought to have let Wildcat write "Your presence is formally requested," after all?

24

The Restaurant

of

Many Orders

Two young gentlemen, dressed just like British military men, with gleaming guns on their shoulders and two dogs like great white bears at their heels, were walking in the mountains where the leaves rustled dry underfoot. They were talking as they went.

"I must say, the country round about is really awful," said one. "Not a bird or beast in sight. I'm just dying to let fly—bang! bang!—at something, anything as long as it moves."

"Oh what fun it would be to let a deer or something have two or three shots smack in his yellow flank!" said the other. "I can just see him spinning round, then flopping down with a thud."

It really was very deep in the mountains. So deep that the professional hunter who had come as their guide

25

went astray and wandered off somewhere. Worse still, the forest was so frightening that the two dogs like white bears both got dizzy. They howled for a while, then foamed at the mouth and died.

"Do you know, I've lost two thousand four hundred silver pieces with this dog," said one young gentleman, casually turning its eyelids back.

"*I've* lost two thousand eight hundred pieces," said the other, tilting his head ruefully on one side.

The first young gentleman went pale.

"I think I'll be getting back," he said, gazing into the other's face.

"Well now," said the other, "I was just beginning to get cold, and hungry as well, so I think I'll be getting back, too."

"Then let's call it a day. What does it matter—on our way back we can call at yesterday's inn and buy a dozen pieces' worth of game birds to take home."

"They had hares too, didn't they? So it'll come to the same thing in the end. Well, why don't we go home, then?"

But it was most annoying. By now, they no longer had the faintest idea of the way back.

A sudden gust of wind sprang up, and the grass stirred, the leaves rustled, and the trees creaked and groaned.

"I really am hungry!" said one. "I've had a dreadfully empty feeling under my ribs for some time."

"So have I," said the other. "I don't feel like walking any farther."

26

"Oh, for something to eat," said the first.

The forest went on stirring and rustling all about them as they were speaking. Just then, one of them happened to look round, and what should he see standing there but a fine brick building. Over the entrance there was a notice that said, in large letters:

RESTAURANT
WILDCAT HOUSE

"Look—this is just right," said one. "The place is civilized after all! Why don't we go in?"

"Funny," said the other, "in a place like this. But I expect we shall be able to get a meal, at any rate."

"Of course we shall, silly. What do you think the sign means otherwise?"

"Why don't we go in? I'm about ready to collapse with hunger."

They stepped into the entrance hall. It was very fine, being done all over in white tiles. There was a glass door, with something written on it in gold letters.

Pray come in, it read. *No one need have a moment's hesitation.*

They were terribly pleased.

"Just look at that!" said one of them. "Things always turn out right in the end. Everything's been going wrong all day, but look how lucky we are now. This place is a restaurant, but they feed you for nothing!"

"I must say, it seems like it," said the other. "That's what 'no one need have a moment's hesitation' means."

They pushed open the door and went through. On the other side was a corridor. Another notice in gold letters on the back of the glass door said:

Plump parties and young parties especially welcome.

They were both overjoyed at this.

"Look, we're especially welcome, it says," said one.

"Because we satisfy both conditions!" said the other.

They walked briskly along the corridor and came to another door, this time painted bright blue.

"What a strange place! I wonder why there are so many doors?"

"This is the Russian way of doing things, of course. It's always like this in cold places or in the mountains."

They were just going to open the door when they saw a notice in yellow letters above it:

We hope you will appreciate that this is a restaurant of many orders.

"Awfully popular, this place. In the mountains like this, too."

"But of course. Why, even in the capital very few of the best restaurants are on the main streets, are they?"

As they were talking, they opened the door. A notice on the other side said:

There are rather a lot of orders, but we hope you will be patient.

"Now just what would *that* mean?" said one young gentleman, screwing up his face.

29

"Mm—I expect it means that there are so many orders that it takes a long time before the food comes, so please forgive us. Something like that."

"I expect so. I want to get settled down in a room as soon as possible, don't you?"

"Yes, and to get seated at a table."

But it was most frustrating—there was yet another door, and by the side of it hung a mirror, with a long-handled brush lying beneath it. On the door it said in red letters:

Patrons are requested to make their hair tidy and to get the mud off their boots here.

"Very proper, too. And only just now in the hall I was thinking this was nothing more than a place for yokels."

"This place is very strict on etiquette. I'm sure they often have very distinguished people here."

So they neatly combed their hair and got the mud off their boots.

But then—no sooner had they put the brush back on its shelf than it blurred and disappeared, and a sudden gust of wind moaned through the room. They huddled together in alarm, and flinging the door open, went into the next room. Both of them were feeling that unless they fortified themselves with something warm to eat very soon, almost anything might happen.

On the other side of the door there was something unexpected written again.

30

Please leave your guns and cartridges here, it said.

Sure enough, there was a black gun-rack right by the door.

"Of course," said one young gentleman, "No one ever ate a meal with his gun."

"I must say, there must be awfully distinguished people here all the time," said the other.

They unshouldered their guns and unbuckled their belts and put them on the rack. Now there was another door, a black one, which said:

> *Be kind enough to remove your hats, overcoats, and boots.*

"What about it—do we take them off?"

"I suppose we'd better. They really must be *very* distinguished people they've got in the back here."

They hung their hats and overcoats on the hook, then took their boots off and padded on through the door. On the other side was the inscription:

> *Please leave your tiepins, cufflinks, spectacles, purses, and everything else metal, especially anything pointed.*

Right by the door, a fine black-painted safe stood open and waiting. It even had a lock on it.

"Ha ha! It seems they use electricity somewhere in the cooking. So metal things are dangerous, especially pointed things—I expect that's what it means."

"I expect so. I wonder if it means you pay the bill on the way out, then?"

31

A. FRANK SMITH. JR. LIBRARY CENTER
SOUTHWESTERN UNIVERSITY
GEORGETOWN, TEXAS 78626

3 3053 00262 9921

"It seems like it, doesn't it?"

"Yes, that must be it."

They took off their spectacles and their cufflinks and so on, put everything in the safe, and clicked the lock shut.

A little further on, they came to another door, with a glass jar standing in front of it. On the door it said:

Please spread cream from the jar all over your face, hands, and feet.

"Why should they want one to put cream on?"

"Well now, it's very cold outside, you know. If it's too warm inside one gets chapped skin, so this is to prevent it. I must say, they seem to be awfully distinguished people in the back. At this rate, we may soon be on speaking terms with the aristocracy!"

They rubbed cream from the jar on their faces, and then on their hands. Then they took their socks off, and rubbed it on their feet as well. Even so, there was still some left, so they both ate some surreptitiously, pretending to be rubbing it on their faces all the while.

Then they opened the door in a great hurry—only to find a notice on the other side which said:

Did you put on plenty of cream? On your ears too?

There was another, smaller jar of cream here.

"Of course—I didn't do my ears. Lucky—I might well have got them chapped. The proprietor of this place is really most thoughtful."

"Yes, he's got an eye for every little detail. Inciden-

tally, I'd like something to eat, but it doesn't look very hopeful with these eternal corridors, does it?"

But the next door was already upon them.

> *The meal will soon be ready*, it said. *We won't keep you as much as fifteen minutes. Make haste and shake some perfume over your head from this bottle.*

And there in front of the door stood a shining gilt perfume bottle.

They splashed perfume over their heads. Unfortunately, though, the perfume smelled dreadfully like vinegar.

"This perfume's awfully vinegary," said one young gentleman. "What's wrong with it, do you suppose?"

"They've made a mistake," the other said. "The maid must have had a cold or something and put the wrong stuff in."

They opened the door and went through. On the other side of the door was a notice in big letters which said:

> *What a wearisome lot of orders, you poor things. There are no more, so be good enough to take some salt from the pot and rub it in well all over you.*

A fine blue china saltcellar was indeed standing there, but this time both the young gentlemen were quite horrified. They turned their cream-smeared faces to look at one another.

"I don't like the look of this," said one.

"Nor do I," said the other.

" 'Lots of orders' means *they're* giving *us* orders."

34

"Yes—and it's my idea that 'restaurant' doesn't mean a place for serving food, but a place for cooking people and serving *them*. And that m-m-means that w-w-we. . ."

But he began to shake and tremble, and tremble and shake, so that he couldn't go on any more.

"Then w-w-we. . . Oh *dear!*" And the other one, too, began to quake and shiver, and shiver and quake, so that he couldn't go on either.

"Let's get out . . ." Still shaking all over, one of the young gentlemen pushed at the door behind him. But strange to say, it refused to budge.

At the other end was another door with two big holes and a silver knife and fork carved on it.

So nice of you to come, it said. *That will do very nicely indeed. Now just pop inside, please.*

What was worse, a pair of blue eyeballs were ogling at them through the keyhole.

"Oh dear!" cried one, quivering and trembling.

"Oh *dear!*" cried the other, trembling and quivering.

And they both burst into tears.

Just then, they heard voices talking furtively on the other side of the door.

"It's no good, they've realized. It doesn't look as if they're going to rub in the salt."

"What d'you expect? The way the boss put it was all wrong, 'You poor things 'n the like—stupid, I calls it."

"Who cares? Either way, *we* won't get as much as the bones even."

"How right you are. But if they won't come in here, it's our responsibility, I tell you."

"Shall we call them? Yes, let's. Hey, gentlemen! This way, quickly. This way. This way! The dishes are washed, and the vegetables nicely salted. All that's left is to combine you properly with the salad and put you on the snowy white dishes. This way now, quickly!"

The two young gentlemen were so distressed that their faces went all crumpled like pieces of waste paper. They peered at each other's faces and shook and shivered and wept silently.

There were chuckles on the other side of the door, then a voice shouted again:

"This way, this way! If you cry like that, you know, you'll wash off all the cream you put on specially. (Yes, sir, coming sir. We'll be bringing it in just a moment, sir.) Come on, this way now!"

"This way, quickly. The boss has his napkin tucked in and his knife in his hand, and he's licking his lips, just waiting for you."

The two young gentlemen just wept and wept and wept and wept.

All of a sudden, there came a "Woof, woof," and a "Grr!" from behind them, and the two dogs like white bears came bursting through the door and into the room. The eyes behind the keyhole disappeared in a twinkling. The dogs rushed round and round the room snarling, then suddenly gave another great woof! and threw themselves at the next door. The door banged open and they rushed inside as though swallowed up. From the pitch darkness beyond came a great miaowing and spitting and growling, then a rustling sound.

The room vanished in a puff of smoke, and the two young gentlemen found themselves standing in the grass shivering and shaking in the cold. Their coats and boots, purses and tiepins were all there too, hanging from the branches or lying among the roots of the trees. There was a gust of wind, the grass stirred, the leaves rustled, and the trees creaked and groaned.

The dogs came back panting for breath, and behind them someone called, "Gentlemen! Gentlemen!"

"Hey! Hey!" they shouted, suddenly recovering their spirits. "We're here. This way, quickly!"

The professional hunter in his straw hat came rustling through the grass, and they really felt safe at last.

They ate the dumplings the guide had brought with him, and they returned to the capital, buying ten pieces' worth of game birds on their way.

But even back in the capital, and however they soaked themselves in hot baths, their faces that had gone all crumpled like waste paper would never go back to normal again.

Nighthawk
and
the Stars

The nighthawk was really a very ugly bird. His face had reddish-brown patches as though someone had daubed it with mud, and his beak was flat, and his mouth stretched right round to his ears. His legs were quite unsteady, and he could barely walk even a couple of yards.

Things were so bad that the other birds only had to look at the nighthawk's face to take a dislike to him. Even the lark, which is not a very beautiful bird, considered itself far better than the nighthawk, and, if it met the nighthawk when he was setting out in the early evening, it would turn its head away with its eyes closed disdainfully, as though he was really too distasteful for words. And the smaller birds who liked to chatter were always saying downright unpleasant things about him.

"Well! Here he comes again," they would say. "Just

look at that my dear! Did you ever see anything like it? It's really a disgrace to us birds!"

"Quite. Why, just look at that great mouth! I'm sure he's related to the frogs."

And so it went on. If only he had been a simple hawk instead of a nighthawk, his name alone would have been enough to send those half-baked little birds into hiding behind the leaves of the trees, all quivering and hunched up, with pale faces. In fact, though, the nighthawk was not a brother of the hawk, not even a relation at all. Surprising to say, he was elder brother to the beautiful kingfisher and to that jewel among birds, the hummingbird. They were all quite harmless to other birds. The hummingbird ate the honey from flowers, and the kingfisher ate fish, while the nighthawk lived by catching winged insects. The nighthawk had no sharp claws or sharp beak even, so that no one, not even the weakest bird, was afraid of him.

It may seem strange that he should have been called "hawk" at all. In fact, there were two reasons. One was that the nighthawk's wings were exceptionally strong, so that when he soared through the air he looked just like a hawk. The other was his voice, which was piercing and also reminded people somehow of the real hawk. Of course, this bothered the real hawk very much. Whenever he so much as caught sight of the nighthawk, he would hunch up his shoulders and call out to him threateningly to get his name changed quickly.

Then, early one evening, the hawk actually visited the nighthawk at his home.

39

"Hey, are you in?" he called. "Haven't you changed your name yet? What a shameless creature you are! Don't you know there's a world of difference between our natures? Why, see how I range the blue skies, while you never come out at all except on cloudy, dark days or at night. And take a look at my beak, too. You'd do well to compare it with your own!"

"I'm afraid I just can't do as you say, Hawk," the nighthawk replied. "I didn't choose my own name. It was given me by God."

"But you're wrong. With *my* name, now, one might say it was given me by God, but yours is kind of borrowed—half from me and half from the night. Give it back!"

"But I *can't*, Hawk."

"Yes, you can! I'll tell you another name instead. Algernon. Algernon—right? Don't you think it's a nice name now? When one changes one's name, of course, one has to have a ceremony to announce it to everybody. You understand? What you do is to go round to everybody's place wearing a sign saying 'Algernon' round your neck, and you bow and you say, 'From now on, I shall be known as Algernon.'"

"Oh, I could never do that!"

"Yes, you could. You've got to! If you don't do it by the morning of the day after tomorrow, I'll crush you to death—remember that! The day after tomorrow in the morning, I'll go round all the other birds' houses and ask whether you've been or not. If there's a single one that says you haven't, that'll be the end of you!"

"But how can you expect me to do such a thing? I'd rather die. So you might as well kill me right now."

"Come, now, think about it more carefully later. Algernon's not half a bad name really." And the hawk spread his great wings out wide and flew off home to his own nest.

The nighthawk sat perfectly still with his eyes shut, thinking. "Why on earth should everybody dislike me so much? I know, really—it's because my face looks as though its been daubed with mud and my mouth is slit from ear to ear. But actually, I've never once done anything bad in all my life. Why, once when a baby white-eye fell out of its nest, I even rescued it and took it back home. But the mother white-eye snatched it back from me just as though she was recovering something from a thief. Then she laughed at me terribly. And now—oh dear!—they want me to wear a sign round my neck saying Algernon! Whatever shall I do . . . ?"

Night was already drawing in about him, and the nighthawk flew out from his nest. The clouds were hanging low and gleaming unpleasantly. The nighthawk nearly brushed against them as he flew noiselessly about the sky.

Suddenly, his mouth opened wide and, setting his wings back straight, he shot down through the sky like an arrow. Insect after insect disappeared down his throat. Then, before you could tell whether he had actually touched the earth or not, he had swung up and was shooting skywards again.

The clouds were gray by now, and a forest fire glowed red on the hills in the distance . . .

Whenever the nighthawk decided to strike, he flew so fast that he seemed almost to split the sky in two. But tonight, among the insects he caught, there was a beetle that struggled dreadfully as it went into his throat. The nighthawk swallowed it down at once, but this time a kind of shudder went down his back as he did so.

Now the clouds were black, except in the east where the forest fire was reflected on them, red and frightening. The nighthawk flew up to the sky again, feeling rather choky in the stomach.

Another beetle went into the nighthawk's maw, but this one flapped about exactly as though it were scratching at his throat. The nighthawk forced it down somehow, but his heart gave a sudden lurch as he did so, and he started crying in a loud voice. Round and round and round the sky he went in circles, crying all the while.

"Oh dear," he was thinking, "here I am every night, killing beetles and all kinds of different insects. And now *I'm* going to be killed by Hawk, and there's only *one* of me. No wonder I feel so miserable. Oh, how wretched! I think I'll stop eating insects, and starve to death. But then, I expect Hawk will kill me before that happens. No—I'll go away, far, far away into the sky before he can get me."

The flames of the forest fire were gradually spreading out like water, and the clouds were red as though ablaze themselves.

The nighthawk flew straight to the home of his younger

42

brother the kingfisher. Luckily enough, the beautiful kingfisher was up too, watching the distant forest fire.

"Good evening, elder brother," he said as he saw the nighthawk flying down towards him. "What business brings you so unexpectedly?"

"To tell the truth, I'm going far away, and I've come to see you before I go."

"But you mustn't, elder brother! Hummingbird lives far away, and you know I shall be left all alone!"

"Well, I'm afraid it can't be helped. Please don't say any more today. And you, too—please be sure not to catch any more fish than is absolutely necessary, won't you? Please. Goodbye."

"What's happened, elder brother? Come, now, don't go just yet!"

"No—it won't make any difference however long I stay. Give Hummingbird my love when you see him, won't you? Goodbye. We shall never meet again. Goodbye."

And he went home weeping. The brief summer night was already giving way to the dawn.

The leaves of the ferns swayed green and cold, drinking in the morning mist. The nighthawk cried out loud and harsh. Then he made his nest neat and tidy, combed every bit of feather and down on his body into place, and set off from his nest again.

The mist cleared, and as it did so the sun climbed from the east. It was so dazzling that the nighthawk wavered for a moment, but he bore with it and flew straight ahead in the direction of the sun.

"Sun, Sun," he called. "Won't you take me up with you? I'll gladly die in your fire if need be. My body may be ugly, yet it will surely give out a tiny light as it burns. Won't you take me up with you?"

But though he flew and flew, the sun grew no closer. In fact, he even seemed to grow smaller and more distant still.

"Nighthawk, eh?" said the sun. "Why, yes—I suppose you do have a hard time. Why don't you fly up into the sky tonight and ask the stars instead? You're really a bird of the night, you see."

The nighthawk gave what was meant to be a bow, but suddenly lost his balance and ended by falling down, down into the grass on the plain below.

For a while, everything was a dream. It seemed to the nighthawk that he was climbing up amidst the red and yellow stars, or that he was being swept away and away by the wind, or that the hawk had come and was crushing him in his claws . . .

Then something cold fell on his face, and he opened his eyes. The dew was dripping from a stem of young pampas grass. It was quite dark, and the deep indigo sky was covered all over with twinkling stars. The nighthawk flew up into the sky. Again tonight the forest fire was gleaming red, and the nighthawk as he flew about found himself between the faint glow from the fire and the cold light of the stars above. Once more he flew round the sky, then suddenly made up his mind and started flying straight upward, toward the constellation of Orion in the western sky.

45

"Oh star!" he called as he went. "Bluish-white star of the west! Won't you take me up with you? I'll willingly die in your fire if need be."

But Orion was too busy singing his brave songs to pay the slightest heed to anything as insignificant as the nighthawk. Unsteadily and nearly weeping, the nighthawk came down till at last he reached a resting place. Once more he flew around the sky. Then off he went straight upwards again, this time towards the Great Dog in the south.

"Oh star!" he cried as he went. "Blue star of the south! Won't you take me up with you? I'll gladly die in your fire if need be."

"Foolish talk!" said the Great Dog, busily winking blue and purple and yellow. "Whatever do you think you are? A mere bird—that's all. Why, to reach here with your wings would take hundreds and thousands and millions of billions of years!" And the Great Dog turned away again.

Disheartened, the nighthawk wavered back down to earth. He flew around the sky twice. Then again he summoned up his resolve and flew straight up in the direction of the Great Bear in the north.

"Oh blue star of the north!" he cried as he went. "Won't you take me up with you?"

"Now, you mustn't say things you shouldn't," said the Great Bear softly. "Go and cool yourself off a little. At times like this, it's best to dive into a sea with icebergs, but if there's no sea near at hand, a cup of water with some ice in it will do nicely."

46

The nighthawk zigzagged dejectedly down to earth again. He flew around the sky four more times. Then he called out once more, to the Eagle, which had just risen on the opposite bank of the Milky Way.

"Oh white star of the east! Won't you take me up with you? I'll happily die in your fires if need be."

"Dear me, no—quite out of the question!" said the Eagle pompously. "One must have the proper social status in order to become a star. And it takes a great deal of money, too."

All his remaining strength left the nighthawk. He folded in his wings, and plummeted down toward the earth. But then, just when his weak legs were only inches from the ground, the nighthawk quite suddenly began to shoot upwards again like a rocket. Up he went, and when he came to the middle regions of the sky, he shook his body and ruffled up his feathers just as an eagle does before it attacks a bear.

He called and called again in a harsh, piercing voice. It was the voice of a hawk, and all the other birds who were asleep on the plains and in the woods below awoke and trembled as they looked up wonderingly at the starry sky.

The nighthawk climbed straight up and up, ever farther up into the sky. Now the flames of the forest fire below were no bigger than a burning cigarette end, yet still he climbed, up and up. His breath froze white on his breast with the cold, and the air grew thinner, so that he had to move his wings more and more frantically to keep going.

Yet the stars did not change their size. The nighthawk wheezed at each breath like a pair of bellows. The cold and the frost pierced him like swords. In the end, his wings went completely numb and useless. Then, with tearful eyes, he gazed once more up into the sky—and that was the last of the nighthawk. No longer did he know whether he was falling or climbing, whether he was facing upwards or downwards. But his heart was at peace now, and his great, bloodied beak, though a little twisted, was surely smiling a little.

A while later, the nighthawk opened his eyes quite clearly, and saw that his own body was burning gently with a beautiful blue light like the flames of blazing phosphorus.

Next to him was Cassiopeia. The bluish-white light of the Milky Way lay just at his back.

And the nighthawk star went on burning. It burned forever and forever.

It is still burning to this day.

The First
Deer
Dance

The setting sun slanted down red on the mossy plain from a gap in the ragged, gleaming clouds in the west, and the swaying fronds of pampas grass shone like white fire. I was tired, and I fell asleep where I was. Gradually, the rustling breeze began to sound to my ears like human speech, and soon it was telling me the true meaning of the Deer Dance that the countryfolk still dance in the hills and on the plain of Kitakami. . . .

Long ago, in the days when the area was still covered all over with tall grass and black forests, Kaju, together with his grandfather and the others, came to live there from somewhere east of the river Kitakami. They settled down there, and cleared the land, and began growing millet.

One day, Kaju fell out of a chestnut tree and hurt his

knee a little. At times such as this, the local folk would go to the mountains to the west where there was a hot spring, and would build a hut there, and bathe in the spring until they were cured.

One fine morning, Kaju, too, set out for the spring. With his rice, his bean paste, and his pot on his back, he walked slowly, limping slightly as he went, across the open country where the fronds of the pampas grass were already blowing silver.

On he went, over streams and across stony wastes, till the mountain range loomed large and clear and he could pick out each single tree on the mountains like the pins on a pincushion. By now the sun was already quite far gone in the west and was glittering with a greenish tinge just above the tops of a clump of a dozen alder trees.

Kaju set the load from his back down on the grass, took out some horse-chestnut and millet dumplings, and began to eat. The pampas grass spread away from him in clump after clump, so many clumps that it seemed to ripple in shining white waves all over the plain. Eating his dumplings, Kaju thought to himself what a fine sight the trunks of the alder trees made, rising quite straight up out of the pampas grass.

But he had walked so energetically that he was too tired to eat. He soon felt full, and in the end, despite himself, he had to leave a piece of dumpling about the size of a horse-chestnut burr.

"I'll leave 'er for the deer," he said to himself. "Deer, do 'ee come and eat!" And he set it down by a small white flower growing at his feet. Then he shouldered his pack once more and slowly, quite slowly, set off again.

But he had only gone a little way when he realized that he had left his cotton towel at the place where he had rested, so he turned back again in a hurry. He could still see the clump of alder trees quite clearly, so to go back was really not much trouble. Yet before he reached the place, he suddenly stopped quite still, sensing beyond all doubt that the deer were already there. And there, indeed, they were—at least five or six, walking towards something, with their moist noses stretched out far in front of them.

Kaju tiptoed softly over the moss towards them, taking care not to brush against the pampas grass.

No mistake about it, the deer had come for the dumpling he had left. "Hah, deer bain't wasting no time," he muttered to himself with a smile, and bending down low, crept slowly in their direction.

He peeped out from behind a clump of pampas grass, then drew back in surprise. Six deer were walking round and round in a ring on the stretch of short grass. Hardly daring to breathe, Kaju peered out at them from between the stems of grass.

The sun had touched the summit of one of the alder trees, and its topmost branches shone with a strange green light, so that it looked for all the world like some green living creature standing stock still, gazing down at the deer. Each frond of pampas grass shone separate and silver, and the deer's fur seemed even shinier and sleeker than usual.

52

Kaju was delighted. He gently lowered himself onto one knee and concentrated on watching the deer.

They were going round and round in a wide circle, but he soon noticed that every one of them seemed intent on something in the center of the ring. He was sure of it, because their heads and ears and their eyes were all pointing in that direction. What was more, now and again one or the other of them would break the circle and stagger a few paces inwards as though drawn towards the center.

Right in the center of the ring, of course, was the horse-chestnut dumpling Kaju had left there a while ago. What was bothering the deer so much, though, was not the dumpling, it seemed, but Kaju's white cotton towel, which lay in a curve where it had fallen on the ground. Bending his bad leg gently with one hand, Kaju sat himself neatly on his heels on the moss in order to watch.

The deer's circling gradually slowed down. Now they trotted gently, every so often breaking out of the ring and putting one foreleg forward towards the center as though about to break into a run, then just as soon drawing back again and trotting on once more. The thudding of their hooves rang pleasantly down into the dark soil of the plain. Finally, they stopped going round and round altogether, and came and stood in a group between Kaju and the towel.

Suddenly, Kaju's ears began to ring and his body began to shake: the same feeling that the deer were feeling, a feeling like fronds of grass swaying in the breeze, was coming over to him in waves. The next moment, he

54

really doubted his own ears, for now he could actually hear the deer talking.

"Shall I go and look, then?" one was saying.

"Naw, 'er be dangerous. Better watch 'er a bit longer."

"Can't get caught with no trick like old fox played on us. 'Er be only a dumpling, when all's said and done."

"Right, right. Only too right."

So the deer's talk went.

" 'Er may be alive."

"Aye, 'er be summat like a living crittur, indeed."

In the end one of them seemed to make up his mind. He straightened his back, left the ring and went in towards the center. All the other deer stopped to watch.

The deer who had gone forward edged towards the towel inch by inch with his neck stretched out just as far as it would go and his legs all bunched up beneath him. Then, quite suddenly, he shot right up in the air and came darting back like an arrow. The other five deer scattered to the four directions, but the first deer stopped dead when he got back to where he had started, so they calmed down and reluctantly came back and gathered in front of him.

"How were it? What do 'er be? That long white thing?"

" 'Er do have wrinkles all the way down 'er."

"Then 'er bain't a living crittur. 'Er be a toadstool or something after all! Poisonous too, I don't doubt."

"Naw, 'er bain't no toadstool. 'Er be a living thing all right."

"Be 'er, now! Alive and lots of wrinkles too—'er be getting on in years, then."

55

"Aye, that sentry guarding the dumpling be a very *elderly* sentry. Oh, ho, ho, ho, ho!"

"Eh, he, he, he, he! A blue and white sentry!"

"Oh, ho, ho, ho, ho! Private Blue-'n-White."

"Shall I go and look now?"

"Do 'ee go, now. 'Er be safe enough."

" 'Er won't bite, now?"

"Naw, 'er be safe, I say."

So another deer crept slowly forward. The five who stayed behind nodded their heads approvingly as they watched.

The deer who had gone forward seemed to be scared to death. Time and time again he bunched his four legs up and arched his back ready for flight, only to stretch them out gingerly and creep forward again the next moment.

At last he reached a spot only a step away from the towel. He stretched his neck out just as far as it would go and went sniff, sniff, at the towel, then suddenly leapt up in the air and came running back. They all started and began to run off, but the first deer stopped dead as soon as he got back, so they took courage and gathered their faces close about his head.

"How were 'er? Why did 'ee run away?"

"But I thought 'er were going to bite I!"

"What *can* 'er be, now?"

"No telling. What be sure is that 'er be white and blue, in patches, like."

"How do 'er smell? Eh, the smell?"

" 'Er do smell like willow leaves."

56

"Do 'er breathe?"

"Now I didn't rightly notice that."

"Shall I go now?"

"Aye, do 'ee go now."

The third deer crept slowly forward. Just then a slight breeze stirred the towel. He halted in his tracks in fright, and the others all started violently. After a while, though, he seemed to calm down, and crept forward again till at last he could stretch the tip of his nose out to the towel.

The five deer left behind were all nodding at each other knowingly. But just then the deer out in front went quite stiff, shot up in the air, and came racing back.

"What did 'ee run away for?"

"Because I had a strange feeling, like."

"Be 'er breathing?"

"Well, I don't rightly think I heard 'er *breathing*. 'Er don't seem to have no mouth, either."

"Do 'er have a head?"

"I couldn't rightly tell about that, either."

"Then shall I go and see this time?"

The fourth deer went out. He was really just as scared as the rest. Even so, he went all the way up to the towel and, ever so boldly, pressed his nose right against it. Then he drew back in a hurry and came dashing back towards them like an arrow.

"Ah, 'er be soft."

"Like mud, would 'er be?"

"Naw."

"Like grass?"

"Naw."

"Like the fur on bean pods?"

"Mm—summat harder than that."

"What could 'er be, now?"

"Any rate, 'er be a living crittur."

" 'Ee think so, after all?"

"Aye, 'er be *sweaty*."

"I'm thinking I'll go and have a look."

The fifth deer in his turn crept forward slowly. This one seemed to be something of a joker, for he dangled his nose right over the towel, then gave his head a great jerk as much as to say "this is very suspicious, now." The other five deer leapt about with amusement.

This encouraged the deer out in front, and he gave the towel a great lick. But then he, too, was suddenly seized with fright, and came dashing back like the wind, with his mouth open and his tongue lolling out. The others were dreadfully startled, too.

"Were 'ee bitten, then? Did 'er hurt?"

But he just shivered and shivered.

"Has your tongue come loose, then?"

Still he shivered and shivered.

"Now, what be up with 'ee? Speak up, now!"

"Phew! Ah! My tongue be all numb, like!"

"What kind of taste do 'er have?"

"No taste."

"Would 'er be alive?"

"I don't rightly know. Do 'ee go and have a look now."

"Aye."

Slowly, the last deer went forward. The others all watched, nodding their heads with interest as he bent down and sniffed at it for a while. Then, quite suddenly, he picked it up in his mouth and came back with it as though there was nothing whatsoever to be afraid of any more. The other deer bounded up and down with delight.

"Well done! Well done! Once we've got 'er, bain't nothing to be afeared of!"

"For sure, 'er be a great dried-up slug."

"Come on now, I'll sing, so do 'ee all dance around 'er."

The deer who had said this went into the middle of the group and began to sing, and the rest began to circle round and round the towel.

They ran and circled and danced, and again and again as they did so one or the other of them would dash forward like the wind and stab the towel with his horns or trample it with his hooves. In no time, Kaju's poor towel was all muddy and holed. Then gradually the deer's circling began to slow down.

"Ah, *now* for the dumpling!"

"Ah, a boiled dumpling 'n all!"

"Ah, 'er be quite round!"

"Ah, yum yum!"

"Ah, wonderful!"

The deer split up and gathered in a ring about the horse-chestnut dumpling. Then they all ate one mouthful of it in turn, beginning with the deer who had gone up to the towel first. The sixth and last deer got a piece hardly bigger than a bean.

Then they formed a ring again, and began to walk

round and round and round in a circle. Kaju had been watching the deer so intently that he almost felt he was a deer himself. He was on the point of rushing out to join them, when he caught sight of his own great, clumsy hand. So he gave up the idea, and went on concentrating on breathing quietly.

Now the sun had reached the middle branches of the alder tree, and was shining with a slightly yellowish light. The deer's dance grew slower and slower. They began nodding to each other busily, and before long they formed up in a line facing the sun, standing perfectly straight as though they were worshiping it. Kaju watched in a dream, forgetful of everything else. Suddenly, the deer at the right-hand end of the line began to sing in a high, thin voice:

See the setting sun decline,
Blazing out behind the leaves
That delicately shine
Green upon the alder tree.

Kaju shut his eyes and shivered all over at the sound of the voice, which was like a crystal flute.

Now the second deer from the right suddenly leapt up and, twisting his body to-and-fro, ran in and out between the others, bowing his head time and time again to the sun till finally he came back again to his own place, stopped quite still, and began to sing:

Now the sun's behind its back
See the leafy alder tree
Like a mirror crack
And shatter in a million lights.

61

Kaju caught his breath and himself bowed low to the sun in his glory, and to the alder tree. The third deer from the right began to sing now, bowing and raising his head busily all the while:

Homeward though the sun may go,
Down beyond the alder tree,
See the grass aglow,
Dazzling white across the plain.

It was true—the pampas grass was all ablaze, like a sea of white fire.

Long and black the shadow lies
On the shimmering pampas grass
Where against the skies
Straight and tall the alder grows.

Now the fifth deer hung his head low, and started singing in a voice that was hardly more than a mutter:

See the sun is sinking low
In the shimmering pampas grass.
Ants now homeward go
Through the moss upon the plain.

Now all the deer were hanging their heads. But suddenly the sixth deer raised his head proudly and sang:

Shy white flower, content to pass
Your days unnoticed in the tall
And shimmering pampas grass—
You are dearest of them all!

Then all the deer together gave a short, sharp call like the cry of a flute, leapt up in the air, and began to dash round and round in a ring.

A cold wind came whistling from the north. The

alder tree sparkled as though it really were a broken mirror. Its leaves actually seemed to tinkle as they touched against each other, and the fronds of the pampas grass seemed to be whirling round and round with the deer.

By now Kaju had forgotten all about the difference between himself and the deer. "Hoh! Bravo, bravo!" he cried, and rushed out from behind the pampas grass.

For one moment the deer stopped stiff and straight in alarm, then the next they were fleeing like leaves before a gale. Their bodies bent forward in haste, breasting the waves of silver pampas grass and the shining sunset, they fled far, far into the distance, leaving the pampas grass where they had passed glittering on and on, like the wake of a boat left on a quiet lake.

Kaju smiled a rueful smile. Then he picked up his muddy, torn towel and set off walking towards the west.

And that was all, until I heard the story from the clear autumn breeze in the late sunlight that day on the mossy plain.

The Earth-god
and
the Fox

1

On the northern edge of a stretch of open land the
ground rose in a slight hillock. The hillock was covered
entirely with spiky-eared grass, and right in the middle
of it stood a single, beautiful female birch tree.

The tree was not actually very big, but its trunk
gleamed a glossy black and its branches spread out
gracefully, and in May its white flowers were like clouds,
while in autumn it shed leaves of gold and crimson and
many other colors.

Birds of passage such as the cuckoo, and the shrike,
and the tiny wren as well, would all come to perch in
the tree. But when a young hawk or some other large
bird was there, the smaller birds would spy him from
afar and refuse to go anywhere near it.

The tree had two friends. One was the Earth-god, who

lived in the middle of a marshy hollow just about five hundred paces away, and the other was a brown fox, who always appeared from somewhere in the southern part of the plain.

Of the two of them it was the fox, perhaps, that the birch tree preferred. The Earth-god, in spite of his imposing name, was too wild, with hair hanging unkempt like a bundle of ragged cotton thread, bloodshot eyes, and his clothes, even, dangling about him like bits of seaweed. He always went barefooted, and his nails were long and black. The fox, on the other hand, was extremely refined and almost never made people angry or offended them.

The only thing was that, if you compared them really carefully, the Earth-god was honest, whereas the fox was, perhaps, just a little dishonest.

2

It was an evening at the beginning of summer. The birch tree was covered all over with soft new leaves, which filled the air about with a delightful fragrance, and the Milky Way was stretched whitish across the sky, and the stars were twinkling and shaking and switching themselves on and off all over the firmament.

On such a night, then, the fox came to pay the birch tree a visit, bringing with him a book of poetry. He was wearing a dark-blue suit fresh from the tailor's, and his light-brown leather shoes squeaked slightly as he walked.

"What a peaceful night!" he said.

"Oh, yes!" breathed the birch tree.

65

"Do you see Scorpio crawling across the sky over there? In China in olden times they used to call the biggest star in the constellation the 'Fire Star,' you know."

"Would that be the same as Mars, now?"

"Dear me, no, it's not Mars. Mars is a *planet*. This one is a real star."

"Then what is the difference between a planet and a star?"

"Why, a planet can't shine by itself. In other words, you see, it has to have light from somewhere else before it can be seen. A star is the kind that shines by itself. The sun, now, is a star of course. He looks big and dazzling to us, but if you saw him from terribly far away, he'd only look like a small star, just the same as the rest."

"Well! So the sun is only one of the stars, is he? Then I suppose the sky must have an awful lot of suns—no, stars—oh silly me, suns—of course?"

The fox smiled magnanimously. "You might put it like that," he said.

"I wonder why some stars are red, and some yellow, and some green?"

The fox smiled magnanimously again and folded his arms loftily across his chest. The book of poetry under his arms dangled perilously, but somehow stopped just short of falling.

"Well, you see," he said, "at first all the stars were like big, fluffy clouds. There are still lots of them like that in the sky. There are some in Andromeda, some in

Orion, and some in the Greyhounds. Some of them are spiral-shaped and some are in rings the shape of fishes' mouths."

"Well now! How I'd like to see them sometime. Stars the shape of fishes' mouths—how splendid!"

"Oh, they are, I can tell you. To tell the truth, I saw them at the observatory."

"Well! How I'd like to see it myself!"

"I'll show you it. To tell the truth, I've a telescope on order from Germany. It'll be here sometime before next spring, so I'll let you have a look as soon as it comes."

The fox had spoken without thinking, but the next moment he thought to himself, "Oh dear, if I haven't gone and told my only friend a fib yet again! But I really didn't mean any harm by it—I only said it to please her. Later on, I'll tell her the whole truth."

The fox was quiet for a while as he thought about this, but the birch tree was too delighted to notice.

"Oh, I'm so happy!" she said. "You're always *so* kind to me."

"Oh, quite," said the fox rather dejectedly. "In fact, I'd do anything so long as it was for you. Won't you read this book of poetry, by the way? It's by a man called Heine. It's only a translation, of course, but it's not at all bad."

"Well, now! May I really borrow it?"

"Of course you may. Pray read it at your leisure . . . Well, I must say goodbye. Bless me, though—I feel there's something I forgot to say."

"Yes—about the color of the stars."

"Why, of course! But let's leave that until next time, shall we? I mustn't impose on your hospitality."

"Oh, *that* doesn't matter."

"I'll be coming again soon, at any rate. Goodbye, then. I'll leave the book with you. Goodbye, now."

The fox went busily off homewards. And the birch tree, its leaves rustling in a south wind that sprang up just then, took up the book of verse and turned the pages in the light of the faint glow from the Milky Way and from the stars dotting the sky. The book contained the "Lorelei" and many other beautiful poems by Heine, and the birch tree read on and on all through the night. Not till something after three, when Taurus was beginning to climb in the east over the plain, did she begin to drowse ever so slightly.

Dawn broke, and the sun rose in the heavens. The dew glittered on the grass, and the flowers bloomed with all their might. Slowly, slowly from the northeast, bathed in the morning sunlight so that he looked as though he had poured molten copper all over himself, came the Earth-god. He came slowly, quite slowly, with his arms folded soberly across his chest.

Somehow, the birch tree felt rather put out, but all the same she shimmered her bright green leaves in the Earth-god's direction as he came, so that her shadow went flutter, flutter, flutter where it fell on the grass. The Earth-god came up quietly and stopped in front of the birch tree.

"Good morning to you, birch tree."

"Good morning."

68

"D'ye know, birch tree, there are so many things I don't understand when I come to think about them. We don't really know very much, do we?"

"Why, what kind of things?"

"Well, take the grass now—why should it be green when it comes out of dark brown soil? And then there are the yellow and white flowers, too. It's beyond me."

"Mightn't it be that the seeds of the grass have green or white inside them already?" said the birch tree.

"Yes. Yes—I suppose that's so," he said. "But even so, it's beyond me. The toadstools in autumn, now—they come up directly out of the soil, without any seeds or anything. And they come up in red and yellow and all kinds of colors, too. It's really beyond me!"

"How would it be if you asked Mr. Fox?" said the birch tree, who was still too infatuated with last night's talk to know any better.

The Earth-god's face suddenly changed color, and he clenched his fists.

"What's that? Fox? What's the fox been saying?"

"Oh," said the birch tree in a faltering voice, "he didn't say anything. It was just that I thought he might know."

"And what makes you think a fox could teach a *god* something? Eh?"

By now the birch tree was so frightened that she could only quiver and quiver. The Earth-god paced about with his arms folded over his chest, gnashing his teeth loudly all the while. Even the grass shivered with fear wherever his jet-black shadow fell on it.

"Fox and his like are a blight on the face of the earth!"

69

he said. "Not a word of truth in 'em, servile and cowardly, and very envious as well! Grr—impudent creature!"

"It will soon be time for the yearly festival at your shrine, won't it?" said the birch tree, recovering her composure at last.

The Earth-god's expression softened slightly.

"That's right," he said. "Today's the third of the month, so there are six days to go."

But then he thought about it for a while, and suddenly he broke out again.

"But human beings are slack and irresponsible! Nowadays they don't bring a single offering for my festival. Why—the next one that sets foot on my territory, I'll drag him down to the bottom of the mud for his pains!"

He stood there grinding his teeth noisily. The birch tree was beside herself at finding that her attempts to soothe him had had just the opposite effect again, and was quite past doing anything except flutter her leaves in the breeze. For a while the Earth-god strode about gnashing his teeth, his arms folded high across his chest and his whole body seeming to blaze as the sunlight poured down on him. But the more he thought about it, the crosser he got, it seemed. In the end, he could bear it no longer and with a great howl rushed violently off home to his hollow.

3

The place where the Earth-god lived was a dank and chilly swamp grown all over with moss and clover and stumpy reeds and, here and there, a thistle or a dreadfully twisted willow tree. There were soggy places where the water seeped through in reddish, rusty patches. You only had to look at it to feel at once that it was all muddy, and somehow frightening.

On a patch like a small island right in the middle of it all stood the Earth-god's shrine, which was about six feet high and made of logs.

The Earth-god came back to the island. He stretched himself out full length on the ground by the side of his shrine, and scratched long and hard at his dark, scraggy legs.

Just then, he noticed a bird flying through the sky right above his head, so he sat up straight and shouted "Shoo!" in a loud voice. The bird wobbled in alarm and for a moment seemed about to fall. Then it fled into the distance, gradually losing height as it went, as though its wings and everything else were paralyzed.

The Earth-god gave a little laugh and got to his feet. But then he happened to glance over in the direction of the hillock, not far away, where the birch tree stood. He suddenly turned pale and his body went as stiff as a poker, and he began to tear at his unkempt hair as though he was too angry for words again.

A solitary woodcutter was coming up from the south of the hollow, striding along the narrow path skirting its edge on his way to work on Mt. Mitsumori. He seemed to know all about the Earth-god, for every now and then he would glance anxiously in the direction of his shrine. But *he*, of course, could not see the Earth-god.

When the Earth-god caught sight of the woodcutter, his face flushed with pleasure. He stretched out his right hand in the woodcutter's direction, then grasped the wrist of his right hand with his left hand and made as though to drag it back towards him. Strange to say, the woodcutter, who thought he was walking along the path all the time, found himself gradually stepping deeper and deeper into the hollow. He quickened his pace as though alarmed, his face turned pale, and his mouth opened and he began to pant.

Slowly, the Earth-god twisted his right fist. And as he did so, the woodcutter gradually began to go round and round in circles. At this he grew more and more alarmed, until finally he was going round and round on the same spot, panting desperately all the while. His only idea seemed to be to get out of the hollow as quickly as he could, but for all his struggles he only managed to circle round in the same place. In the end he began to cry nervously, and flinging up his arms started to run.

This seemed to delight the Earth-god. He went on grinning and watching without getting up from the ground, until before long the woodcutter—who by now was quite tired and giddy—collapsed in the water. Then the Earth-god got slowly to his feet. With long strides he squelched his way over to where the woodcutter lay and, picking him up, flung him over onto the grassy ground. The woodcutter landed in the grass with a thud. He groaned once and stirred, but still did not come to.

The Earth-god laughed out loud. His laughter rose up into the sky in great, mysterious waves. Reaching the

sky, the sound bounded back and came down again to the place where the birch tree stood. The birch tree suddenly turned so pale that the sunlight shone green through her leaves, and she began to quiver frantically.

The Earth-god tore at his hair with both hands. He thought to himself, "It's all because of the fox that I feel so miserable. Or rather, the birch tree. No—the fox *and* the birch tree. That's why I have such a hard time. If only I didn't mind about the birch tree, I'd mind even less about the fox. I may be nobody much, but I *am* a god after all, and it's disgraceful that I should have to bother myself about a mere fox. But the awful thing is, I do. Why don't I forget all about the birch tree, then? Because I can't. How splendid it was this morning when she went pale and trembled! I was wrong to bully a wretched human being just to work off my crossness, but it can't be helped. Nobody can tell *what* he'll do when he gets really cross."

He felt so dreadfully sad that he beat at the air in despair. Another hawk came flying through the sky, but this time the Earth-god just watched him go in silence.

From far, far away came the sound of cavalry at their maneuvers, with a crackling of rifle-fire like salt being thrown on the fire. From the sky, the blue light poured down in waves. It must have done the woodcutter good, for he came to, sat up fearfully, and peered all about him. The next moment he was up and running away like an arrow from a bow. Off he ran like an arrow, in the direction of Mt. Mitsumori.

Watching him, the Earth-god again gave a great laugh.

74

Again his laughter soared up to the blue sky and hurtled back down on the birch tree below. Again the birch tree's leaves went pale and she trembled delicately, so delicately you would scarcely have noticed.

The Earth-god walked aimlessly round and round his shrine till finally, when at last he seemed to feel more settled, he darted suddenly inside it out of sight.

4

It was a misty night in August. The Earth-god was so terribly lonely and so dreadfully cross that he left his shrine on an impulse and started walking. Almost before he realized it, his feet were taking him in the direction of the birch tree. He couldn't say why, but whenever he thought of the birch tree his heart seemed to turn over and he felt intolerably sad. Nowadays he was feeling very much better than before, so he had tried his best not to think about the fox or about the birch tree, but, try as he might, they kept coming into his mind. Every day he would tell himself over and over again, "You're a god after all—what can a single birch tree mean to you?" Yet even so, he still felt awfully sad. The memory of the fox, in particular, hurt so much that it felt just as though his whole body was on fire.

Wrapped in his own thoughts, the Earth-god drew nearer and nearer to the birch tree. Finally it dawned on him quite clearly that he was on his way to see her—and his heart began to dance for joy. It had been so long since the last time that the birch tree might well be missing him. In fact, the more he thought about it the surer he felt it was so. If it was really so, then he felt very sorry for neglecting her. His heart danced as he strode on through the grass. But before long his stride faltered and he stopped dead, as though a great, blue wave of sadness had suddenly washed over him. The fox was there before him. It was quite dark by now, but he could hear the fox's voice coming through the mist, which was glowing in the vague light of the moon.

"Why, of course," he was saying. "Just because something agrees with the laws of symmetry is not to say that it is beautiful. That's nothing more than a dead beauty."

"How right you are!" came the birch tree's soft voice.

"True beauty is not something rigid and fossilized. People talk of observing the laws of symmetry, but it's enough if only the *spirit* of symmetry is present."

"Oh, yes, I'm sure it is," came the birch tree's gentle voice again.

This time the Earth-god felt as though red flames were licking over his whole body. His breath came in short gasps, and he really thought he could bear it no longer. "What are you so miserable about?" he asked himself crossly. "What is it after all but a bit of talk between a birch tree and a fox in the middle of a plain? Do you call yourself a god, to let such things upset you?" But the fox was talking again:

". . .so all books on art touch on this aspect."

"Do you have many books on art, then?" asked the birch tree.

"Oh, not such an enormous number. I suppose I have

76

most of them in English, German, and Japanese. There's a newer one in Italian, but it hasn't come yet."

"Oh, how *fine* your library must be!"

"No, no—just a few scattered volumes, you know. And besides, I use it for my studies too, so it's really an awful mess, what with a microscope in one corner, and the *London Times* lying over there, and a marble bust of Caesar here . . ."

"Oh, but how splendid! Really *splendid*!"

There was a little sniff from the fox which might have been either modesty or pride, then everything was still for a while.

By now the Earth-god was quite beside himself. From what the fox said, he was actually more distinguished than the Earth-god himself. Now he could no longer console himself by telling himself that he was a god if nothing else. Oh, it was frightful—he felt like rushing over and tearing the fox in two. He told himself that one should never even *think* such things. But then, what was he to do? Hadn't he let the fox get the better of him? He clutched at his breast in his distress.

"Hasn't the telescope you once mentioned come yet?" started the birch tree again.

"The telescope I mentioned?—oh, no, it hasn't come yet. I keep expecting it, but the shipping routes are terribly busy. As soon as it comes, I'll bring it for you to see. I really must show you the rings round Venus for one thing—they're so beautiful."

At this, the Earth-god clapped his hands over his ears and rushed off to the north like an arrow from a

77

bow. He had suddenly got scared at the thought of what he might do if he stayed silent there any longer.

He ran on and on in a straight line. When he finally collapsed out of breath he found himself at the foot of Mt. Mitsumori.

He rolled about in the grass, tearing at his hair. Then he began to cry in a loud voice. The sound rose up into the sky, where it echoed like thunder out of season and made itself heard all over the plain. He wept and wept until dawn when, tired out, he finally wandered vacantly back to his shrine.

5

Time passed, and autumn came at last. The birch tree was still green, but on the grass round about, the golden ears were already formed and glinting in the breeze, and here and there the berries of the lily-of-the-valley showed ripe and red.

One transparent gold autumn day found the Earth-god in the very best of tempers. All the unpleasant things he had been feeling since the summer seemed somehow to have dissolved into a kind of mist that hovered in only the vaguest of rings over his head. The funny, cross-grained streak in him had gone right away, too, and he felt that if the birch tree wanted to talk to the fox—well, she could, and that if the two of them enjoyed talking together then it was a very good thing for them both. He would let the birch tree know how he felt today.

With a light heart and his head full of such thoughts,

the Earth-god set out walking in the direction of the birch tree.

The birch tree saw him coming in the distance, and as ever she trembled anxiously as she waited for him to arrive.

The Earth-god came up and greeted her cheerfully:

"Good morning, birch tree. A lovely day we're having!"

"Good morning, Earth-god. Yes, it's a lovely day."

"What a blessing the sun is, to be sure! There he is up there, red in the spring, white in the summer, and golden in the autumn, and when he turns golden in the autumn the grapes turn purple. Ah, a blessing indeed!"

"How true!"

"D'ye know—today I feel so much better about things. I've had all kinds of things to try me since the summer, but this morning at last something suddenly lifted from my mind."

The birch tree wanted to reply, but for some reason a great weight seemed to be bearing down on her, and she remained silent.

"The way I feel now, I'd willingly die for anybody. I'd even take the place of a worm if it had to die and didn't want to." He gazed into the blue sky in the distance as he spoke, his eyes dark and splendid.

Again the birch tree wanted to reply, but again something heavy seemed to weigh her down, and she barely managed a sigh.

It was then that the fox appeared.

When the fox saw the Earth-god there, he started and

turned pale. But he could hardly go back, so he came, trembling slightly, right up to where the birch tree stood.

"Good morning, birch tree," said the fox. "I believe that's the Earth-god I see there, isn't it?"

He was wearing his light-brown leather shoes and a brown raincoat, and was still in his summer hat.

"I'm the Earth-god. Lovely weather, isn't it?" The Earth-god spoke without a shadow on his mind.

"I must apologize for coming when you have a visitor," said the fox to the birch tree, his face pale with jealousy. "Here's the book I promised you the other day. Oh, and the telescope—I'll show you it one evening when the sky's clear. Goodbye."

"Oh, thank you so much. . ." said the birch tree, but the fox had already set off back home, without so much as a nod to the Earth-god. The birch tree went suddenly pale and began to quiver again.

For a while, the Earth-god gazed vacantly after the fox's retreating form. Then the sun suddenly glinted on the fox's brown leather shoes amidst the grass, and he came to himself with a start. The next moment, something seemed to click in his brain. The fox was marching steadily into the distance, swaggering almost defiantly as he went. The Earth-god began to seethe with rage. His face turned a dreadful black color. He'd show him what was what—that fox with his art books and his telescopes!

He was up and after the fox in a flash. All the birch tree's branches began to shake at once in panic, and the fox himself, sensing something wrong, glanced

80

round casually, only to see the Earth-god, black all over, rushing after him like a hurricane. Off went the fox like the wind, his face white and his mouth twisted with fear.

To the Earth-god, the grass all about seemed to be burning like white fire. Even the shining blue sky had suddenly become a yawning black pit with crimson flames burning and roaring in its depths.

They ran snorting and panting like two railway trains. The fox ran as in a dream, and all the while part of his brain kept saying, "This is the end. This is the end. Telescope. Telescope. Telescope . . ."

A small hummock of bare earth lay ahead. The fox dashed round it so as to get to the round hole at its base. He ducked his head, and was diving into the hole, his back legs flicking up as he went, when the Earth-god finally pounced on him from behind. The next moment he lay all twisted, with his head drooping lifelessly over the Earth-god's hand and his lips puckered as though smiling slightly.

The Earth-god flung the fox down on the ground and stamped on his soft, yielding body some four or five times. Then he plunged into the fox's hole.

It was quite bare and dark, though the red clay of the floor had been trodden down hard and neat.

The Earth-god went outside again feeling rather strange, with his mouth gaping all wide and twisted. Next, he tried putting a hand inside the pocket of the fox's raincoat as he lay there dead and limp. The pocket contained two brown burrs, of the kind foxes comb their fur with. From the Earth-god's open mouth came the most extraordinary sound, and he burst into tears.

The tears fell like rain on the fox, and the fox lay there dead, with his head lolling limper and limper and the faintest of smiles on his face.

The
Red
Blanket

The Old Snow Woman was away, far away. With her pointed ears like a cat's and her swirling ashen hair, she was far, far away beyond the ragged gleaming clouds over the western mountains.

Wrapped in a red blanket, a solitary child was hurrying impatiently home past the foot of a snow-covered hillock the shape of a great elephant's head, his mind full of thoughts of homemade candy.

I'll make a cone of newspaper, he told himself, *and I'll puff and puff till the charcoal burns up bright and blue. Then I'll put a handful of brown sugar in the candy pan, and then a handful of crystal sugar. Then I'll add some water, and all that'll be left will be to boil it, bubble, bubble, bubble . . .*

84

No doubt about it, he had no thought for anything but homemade candy as he hurried on his way home.

All the while, up there in the cold, crystal-clear regions of the sky, the sun was busy stoking his dazzling white fire. The light from it shone out in all directions. Some of it came falling down to earth, and transformed the snows on the hushed uplands into a dazzling sheet of white icing.

Near the top of the hillock that was shaped like an elephant's head, two snow wolves were walking, with their bright red tongues lolling. Snow wolves are invisible to human beings, but once the wind has set them raging, they will leap up off the snow at the edge of the uplands and, treading the swirling clouds of snow, rush hither and thither about the sky.

"To heel! Didn't I tell you not to go too far away?" came a voice behind the snow wolves.

It was the Snow Boy, who came walking slowly with his three-cornered cap of polar-bear fur set on the back of his head and his face ruddy like an apple.

The snow wolves shook their heads and wheeled round, then were off again panting, with their bright red tongues lolling. The Snow Boy gazed up at the bright blue sky and called to the invisible stars beyond it. The blue light pulsed down in steady waves from the sky, and the snow wolves were already far away in the distance, their bright red tongues darting like flames.

"To heel, I said, to heel!" cried the Snow Boy, dancing with rage till his shadow, which had lain clear and black on the snow, changed to a gleaming white light and the wolves came darting back in a straight line with ears pricked.

Swift as the wind, the Snow Boy climbed up the hill that was shaped like an elephant's head. The snow on the hill was raised in lumps like seashells by the wind, and at its summit stood a great chestnut tree with mistletoe growing on it in beautiful golden globes.

"Fetch me some!" ordered the Snow Boy as he climbed the hill. At the first flash of his master's small white teeth, one of the wolves had bounced like a ball into the tree and was chewing at the small branch bearing the golden berries. His shadow fell far and wide over the snow as his head moved busily to-and-fro up in the tree. In no time, the green bark and yellow pith of the branch were ripped through, and it fell at the Snow Boy's feet just as he reached the top of the hill.

"Thank you," said the Snow Boy. As he picked it up, his gaze swept over to the handsome town standing far away on the white and indigo plain. The river glittered, and white smoke rose from the railway station. The Snow Boy dropped his gaze to the foot of the hill. Along the narrow path through the snow that skirted it, the child in the red blanket was hurrying intently towards his home in the hills.

"That's the one who was pushing the sleigh of charcoal yesterday," thought the Snow Boy. "He's bought himself some sugar and is coming back alone."

He laughed, and flicked the sprig of mistletoe he held in his hand toward the child. It flew straight as a bullet and landed before the child's very nose.

86

The child was startled. He picked up the branch and looked all about him wide-eyed. The Snow Boy laughed and cracked his whip. Then from all over the cloudless, polished, deep blue sky, white snow began to fall like feathers from a snowy heron. It made that quiet, lovely Sunday of snow on the plain below, of amber light and brown cypress trees, still more beautiful than ever. The child began to walk as fast as he could, still clutching the mistletoe in his hand.

But then, just as this harmless snow stopped falling, the sun seemed somehow to move farther away in the sky to the resting-place where he replenished his dazzling white fires. From the northwest a slight breeze sprang up. The sky had turned bitterly cold. From far off to the east, in the direction of the sea, there came a tiny sound as though something had slipped in the sky's mechanism, and small shapes seemed to pass rapidly across the face of the sun, which by now was a great white mirror.

The Snow Boy tucked his leather whip under his arm, folded his arms tightly, pressed his lips together, and gazed steadily in the direction from which the wind was blowing. The wolves stretched their necks out straight and gazed intently in the same direction.

The wind grew steadily stronger, and the snow at their feet streamed back away from them with a steady rustling. Soon what looked like a column of white smoke was to be seen standing on the peaks of the distant mountain range, and all at once the west was everywhere dark and gray.

The Snow Boy's eyes blazed fiercely. The sky turned

white all over, the wind seemed to be tearing everything apart, and the snowflakes came, dry and powdery. Now the air was full of ashen snow, though whether it was really snow or cloud would have been hard to tell.

The ridges of the hills began all at once to give out a sound, a kind of creaking and swishing. The horizon and the town disappeared beyond the dark vapor, leaving only the white shape of the Snow Boy, dimly visible as he stood erect in the storm.

Then, from amidst the rending and howling of the wind, there came another, stranger voice:

"Whew! Why do you tarry? Come, snow! Whew! Whew! Come, snow! Come, blow! Why do you tarry? Is there no work to do? Wheew! Wheew! Have I not brought three with me from yonder? Come, snow! Whew!"

The Snow Boy leapt up as though electrified. The Old Snow Woman had arrived.

Crack! went the Snow Boy's whip, and the snow wolves bounded forward all together. His face went pale, his lips tightened together, and his hat flew away in the wind.

"Whew! Whew! To work, now! No idling! Whew! Whew! To work, then! To work! Whew!"

The Old Snow Woman's swirling cold white locks spun round and round in the snow and wind, and her pointed ears and glittering gold eyes were visible among the scurrying black clouds. The three snow boys she had brought with her from the western plain were already rushing to-and-fro unceasingly, with faces deadly pale and lips clamped tight, too busy even to exchange

88

greetings with one another. By now hills and driving snow and sky were quite undistinguishable, and the only sounds were the yells of the Old Snow Woman as she went to-and-fro, the cracking of the snow boys' whips, and the panting of the nine snow wolves as they rushed about in the newly fallen snow.

But then, in the midst of it all, the Snow Boy happened to hear the voice of the child, crying. An odd light gleamed in his eyes. He stopped for a moment and thought. Then, cracking his whip fiercely, he rushed off to find the child.

He must have mistaken the direction, for he collided with a black, pine-clad hill far off to the south. He tucked his whip under his arm and pricked up his ears.

"Whew! Whew!" came the Old Snow Woman's voice. "I'll have no idling! Come, snow! Snow! Come, whew! Whew! Whew, whew! Whew!"

Once more, from amidst the raging of the wind and the snow, he caught the transparent sound of a child crying. Straight as a die, the Snow Boy ran over in its direction, the Old Snow Woman's dishevelled locks wrapping themselves unpleasantly round his face as he went. There, amidst the snow on the pass over the hills, was the child in the red blanket, alone in the raging storm where he had toppled over with his feet stuck firmly in the snow. He was crying and thrusting one hand into the snow in an effort to get himself up.

"Lie back and pull the blanket over you!" shouted the Snow Boy as he ran. "Lie back and pull the blanket over you. Whew!"

But the child heard only the voice of the wind, and could see nothing.

"Fall over on your back," cried the Snow Boy, running back again. "Whew! You mustn't move. It will soon be over, so lie back with the blanket over you!"

But the child was still struggling to get up.

"Fall down!" cried the Snow Boy, rushing past again. "Whew! Be quiet and fall down on your back! It's not so cold today, you won't freeze."

Again the child tried to get up, weeping all the while, his mouth twisted and trembling with fear.

"Lie down! Oh, it's no use!" And the Snow Boy deliberately gave the child a great buffeting, so that he fell over.

"Whew!" The Old Snow Woman had come up. "Harder to work! No idling, now! On, on! Whew!" He could see her purple slit of a mouth and her pointed teeth looming through the storm. "Ohoh! Here's a funny child! That's right! We'll have him. Why—we've a right to take one or two at least at this time of year."

"Of course we have," said the Snow Boy. "Here, that'll finish you!" And he deliberately gave the child another buffeting. But softly he whispered to him, "Lie still. You mustn't move, do you hear?"

The snow wolves were still rushing about as though they were mad, their black paws darting in and out of sight amidst the whirling snow. "Well done! That's right!" cried the Old Snow Woman as she flew off in the other direction again. "Come, snow! I'll have no idling. Whew!" The child tried again to get up. Laughing, the

Snow Boy gave him another great buffeting. By now everything had gone dim and murky. Although it was not yet three in the afternoon it seemed as though the sun had already set. The child's strength had given out, and he did not try to get up any more. Laughing, the Snow Boy stretched out a hand and pulled the red blanket right over him.

"Now go to sleep. I'll cover you with many quilts, so you'll not freeze. Dream now of homemade candy till the morning."

Over and over again he repeated the words as he piled layer after layer of snow on the child. Soon the red blanket had disappeared, and the snow above it was smooth and even all over.

"That child still has the mistletoe I gave him," muttered the Snow Boy to himself, looking tearful for a moment.

"To work, to work!" came the Old Snow Woman's voice through the wind from afar. "No rest for us today until two in the morning. No rest for us today! Come, snow! Whew! Whew-whew! Whew!"

At last, amidst wind and snow and ragged gray clouds, the sun really did set. All through the night the snow fell and fell and fell. Then, when dawn was near, the Old Snow Woman rushed one last time straight through from south to north.

"Come, take your rest," she cried. "I must away to the sea again. None need follow me. So rest your fill and prepare for our next meeting. My, my, how well it went! A good day it was!"

Her eyes shone in the darkness with a strange blue light, and she rushed off to the east with her rough, dry hair swirling and her mouth chattering.

Now plain and hills seemed to relax, and the snow shone with a bluish-white light. The sky had cleared, and the starry constellations were twinkling all over the deep blue heavens.

The snow boys collected their wolves and greeted each other for the first time.

"Terrific today, wasn't it?"

"Mm."

"Wonder when we shall meet again?"

"I wonder. But not more than twice again this year, I expect."

"I'm longing for us all to go home north together."

"Mm."

"A child died a while ago, didn't he?"

"It's all right. He's only asleep. Tomorrow I'll leave a mark there to show where he is."

"We'd better go. Have to be back beyond the hills by dawn."

"Goodbye, then."

"Goodbye."

The three snow boys with their nine wolves set off homewards to the west. Before long, the eastern sky began to shine like a yellow rose, then gleamed amber, and finally flared up all gold. Everywhere, hills and plain alike, was full of new snow.

The Snow Boy's wolves were sitting limp and exhausted. The Snow Boy, too, sat down on the snow and laughed.

94

His cheeks were like apples and his breath had the fragrance of lilies.

The gleaming sun rose in all his glory, with a bluish tinge today that made him more splendid than ever. The whole world flooded pink with sunlight. The snow wolves got up and opened wide their mouths from which the blue flames flickered.

"Come, all of you, follow me," said the Snow Boy. "Dawn has broken, we must wake the child."

He ran to where the child was buried beneath the snow.

"Here, scratch away the snow just here," he ordered.

With their back legs, the snow wolves kicked up the snow, which the breeze scattered at once like smoke.

A figure wearing furs, with snowshoes on its feet, was hurrying from the direction of the village.

"That will do!" shouted the Snow Boy, seeing the edge of the child's red blanket peeping out from under the snow.

"Your father is coming," he cried, racing up the hillock in a column of powdery snow. "You must wake up now!"

The child seemed to stir a little. And the figure in furs came running for all it was worth.